HOW TO
BE KIND
IN KINDERGARTEN
A Book for Your Backpack

To my mother and father,
who taught me kindness—DJS

To my grandma, Rhin, for always
supporting and encouraging me—RH

GROSSET & DUNLAP
An Imprint of Penguin Random House LLC, New York

Text copyright © 2021 by David Steinberg. Illustrations copyright © 2021 by Ruth Hammond. All rights reserved. Published by Grosset & Dunlap, an imprint of Penguin Random House LLC, New York. GROSSET & DUNLAP is a registered trademark of Penguin Random House LLC. Manufactured in China.

Visit us online at www.penguinrandomhouse.com.

Library of Congress Cataloging-in-Publication Data is available upon request.

ISBN 9780593226728 (pbk)
ISBN 9780593226940 (hc)

10 9 8 7 6 5 4 3
10 9 8 7 6 5 4 3 2 1

HOW TO BE KIND
IN KINDERGARTEN

A Book for Your Backpack

BY
D. J. STEINBERG

ILLUSTRATED BY
RUTH HAMMOND

GROSSET & DUNLAP

Are *you* in kindergarten?
Is that really true?
How in the world did you get so big?
So smart and funny, too!

How did you get such a great big heart?
And look at that great big mind!
Put those together and what do you get?
A kid who knows how to be kind!

Hooray for Kindergarten!

Whenever anyone needs a hand,
three guesses who will be there.
YOU!
'Cause you're the kind of kid
who always shows you care.

If a kindergarten friend looks sad,
do you just skedaddle along?
Of course not!
You're a kind kid—
the kind who stops and asks what's wrong.

And when you see someone watching
who's too shy to join in,
you always include him in your game,
'cause you know that's the biggest win!

When someone has different clothes or food,
do you stare or make silly faces?
NO WAY!
You love to share and learn
all about other cultures or places.

When someone wants your scooter
at playtime in the yard,
you're a world pro at taking turns
(even though it can be hard).

If a friend's out sick from school,
and you all hope she feels better,
the class sends out kind wishes
in a handmade get-well letter!

Look—there's a new kid at school today!
Remember when you were new, too?
You march on over to say hello,
'cause that's just what kids like you do.

Aa Bb Cc Dd Ee Ff Gg Hh Ii Jj

Paper   Crayon

What does a kind kindergartner do
when you see a wet kinder-fella
sloshing along in the pouring rain
without his own umbrella?

Say you have two fuzzy mittens,
but your friend at school has none—
what do you do?
Do you share your pair,
so that each of you has one?

Kindness is when the class has a party,
and somebody's cupcake goes *SPLAT!*
and you haven't eaten your own cupcake yet—
would you offer up half of that?

Do kind kids ever make mistakes?
You'd better believe they do!
Sometimes words can hurt feelings,
even though they didn't *mean* to.

Do kind kids say "I'm sorry"
when they see that someone's upset?
They do!
And sometimes, if people say "sorry" to you,
do you forgive them?
You bet!

Kindness is when you are kind for no reason
but simply because it feels good!
Kindness is doing nice things 'cause you want to
and not just because you should.

So hip hip hooray for kindness!
Let's hear it for kids just like *you*,
for making the world so much kinder each day
with all the kind things that you do!